If I were you
I wouldn't look
Because this is . . .

For Carol from Tim

Library of Congress Cataloging in Publication Data

Crowley, Arthur.

The ugly book.

Summary: Ugliness can be seen in everything
around us, from butterflies and flowers to the
moon and stars, if one is looking for it.

[1. Stories in rhyme.   2. Ugliness—Fiction]
I. Gusman, Annie, ill.   II. Title.
PZ8.3.C8863Ug   [E]   81-17863
ISBN 0-395-31858-0   AACR2

Text copyright © 1982 by Arthur Crowley
Illustrations copyright © 1982 by Annie Gusman

Printed in the United States of America
H   10 9 8 7 6 5 4 3 2 1

THE UGLY BOOK

Written by Arthur Crowley

Illustrated by Annie Gusman

Houghton Mifflin Company   Boston   1982

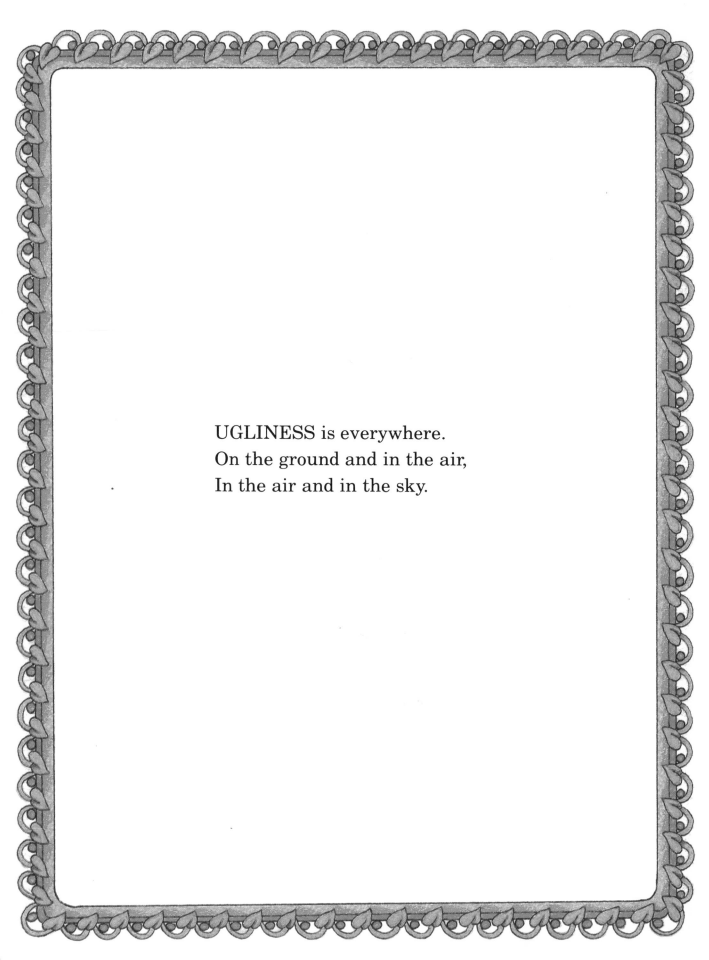

UGLINESS is everywhere.
On the ground and in the air,
In the air and in the sky.

Oh, look! An ugly BUTTERFLY!

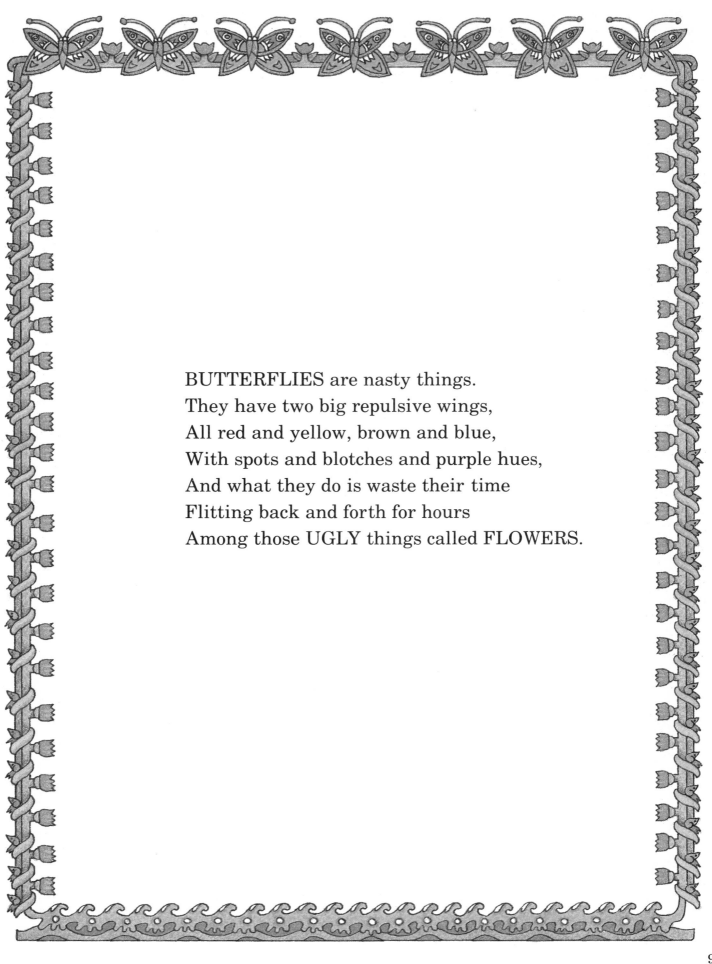

BUTTERFLIES are nasty things.
They have two big repulsive wings,
All red and yellow, brown and blue,
With spots and blotches and purple hues,
And what they do is waste their time
Flitting back and forth for hours
Among those UGLY things called FLOWERS.

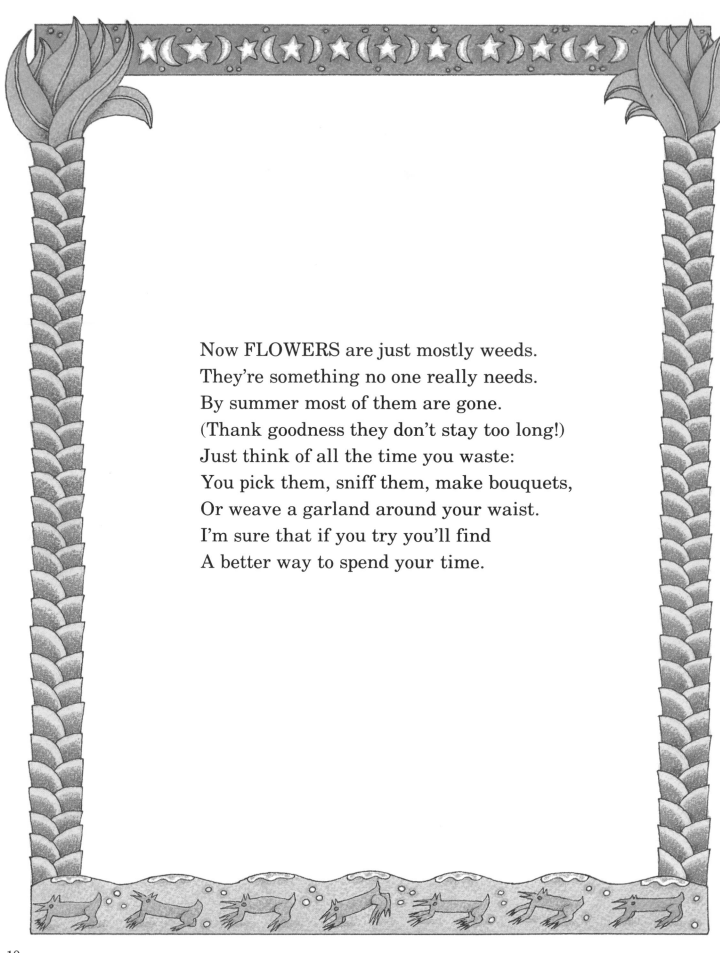

Now FLOWERS are just mostly weeds.
They're something no one really needs.
By summer most of them are gone.
(Thank goodness they don't stay too long!)
Just think of all the time you waste:
You pick them, sniff them, make bouquets,
Or weave a garland around your waist.
I'm sure that if you try you'll find
A better way to spend your time.

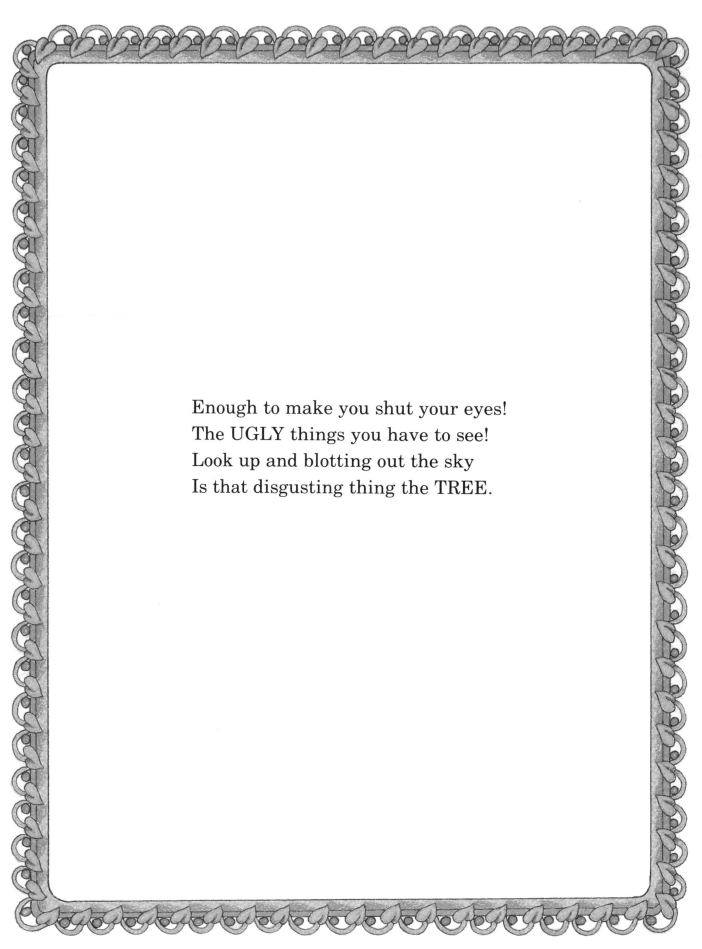

Enough to make you shut your eyes!
The UGLY things you have to see!
Look up and blotting out the sky
Is that disgusting thing the TREE.

13

With knots and bark and limbs and leaves
(nevermind the shade it gives),
But worst of all a TREE provides
A place for horrid *beasts* to live.

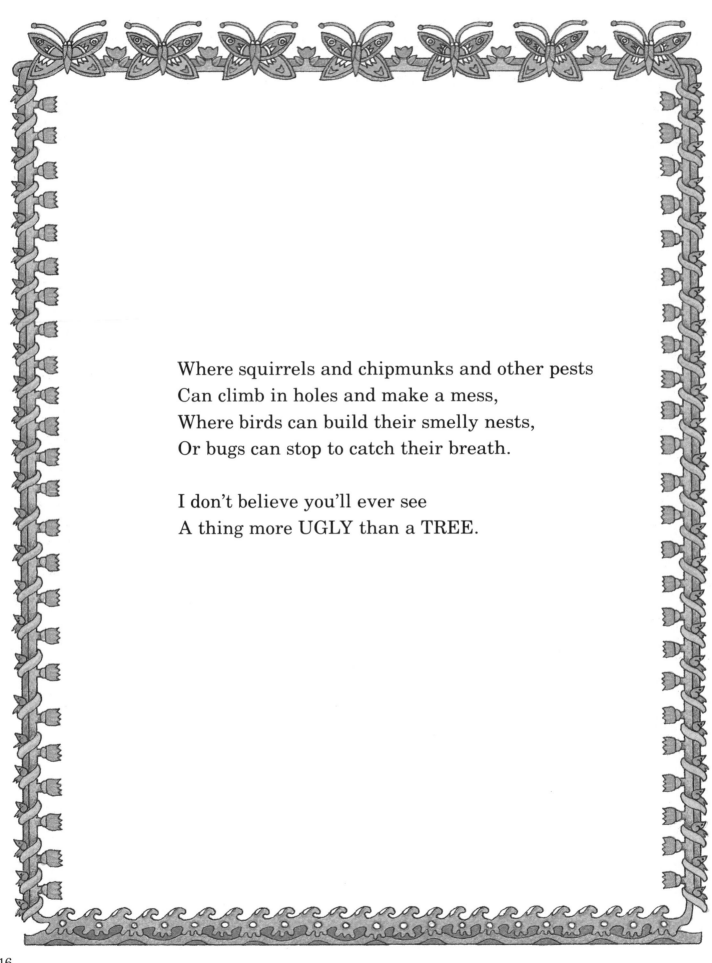

Where squirrels and chipmunks and other pests
Can climb in holes and make a mess,
Where birds can build their smelly nests,
Or bugs can stop to catch their breath.

I don't believe you'll ever see
A thing more UGLY than a TREE.

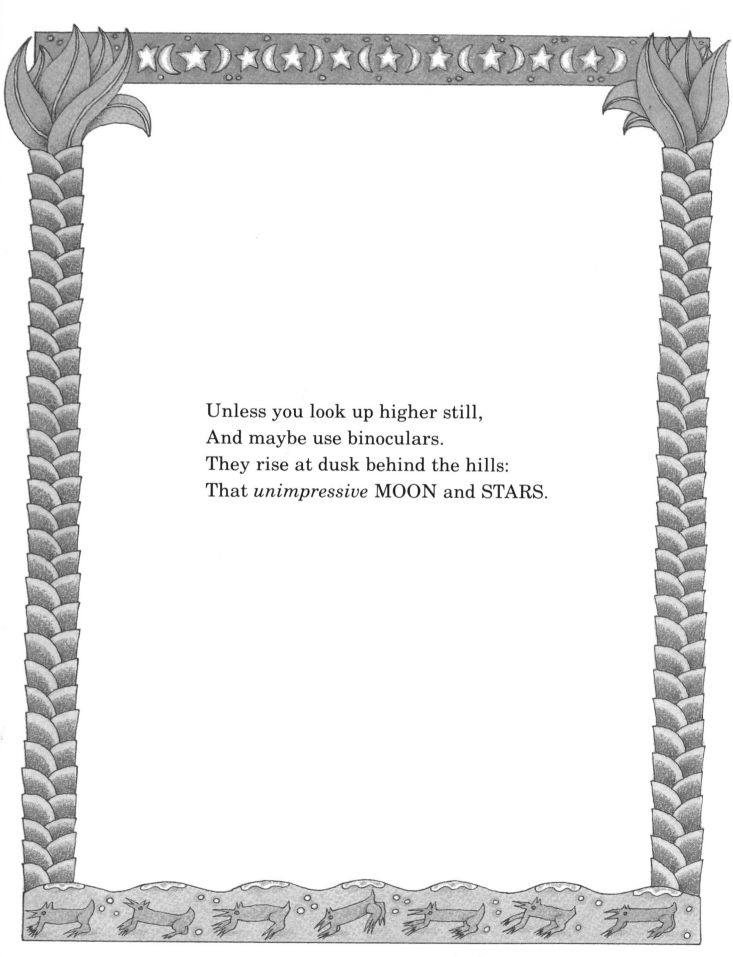

Unless you look up higher still,
And maybe use binoculars.
They rise at dusk behind the hills:
That *unimpressive* MOON and STARS.

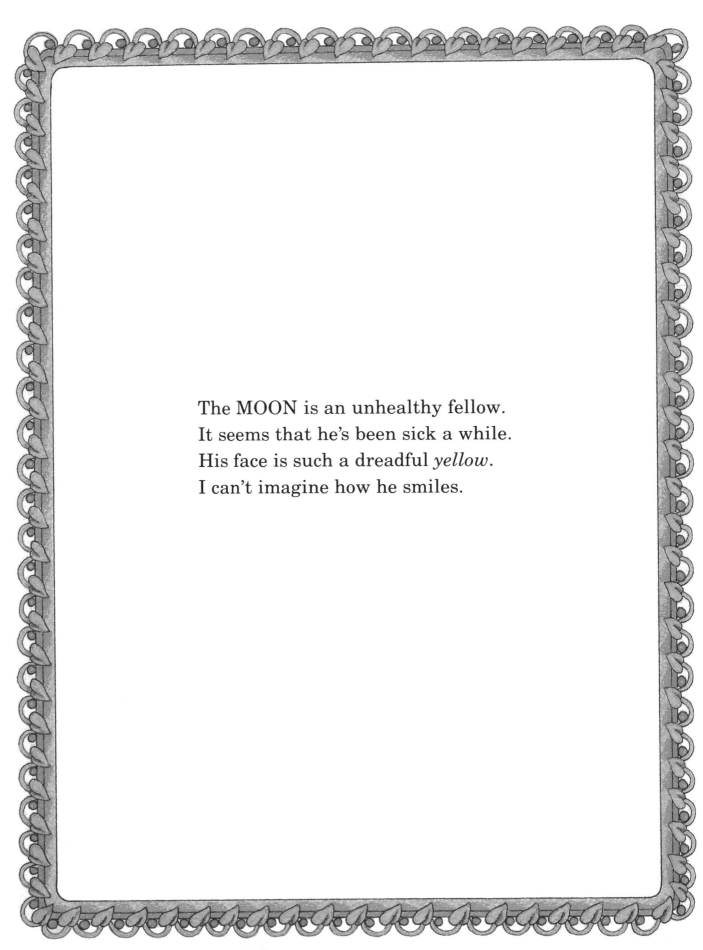

The MOON is an unhealthy fellow.
It seems that he's been sick a while.
His face is such a dreadful *yellow*.
I can't imagine how he smiles.

The STARS? They're just ten billion lights
That clutter up the universe.

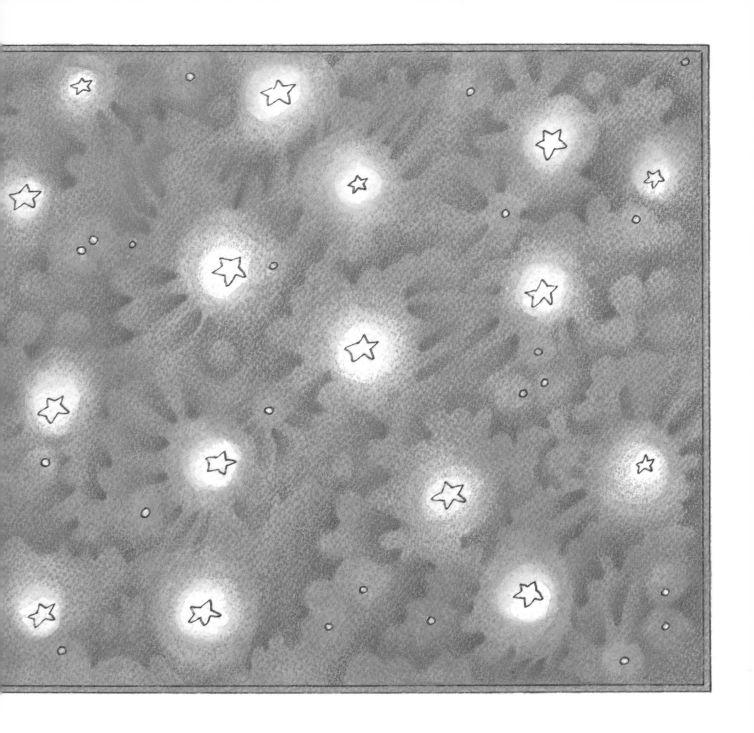

Not a very pretty sight.
And all that twinkling gets on my nerves.

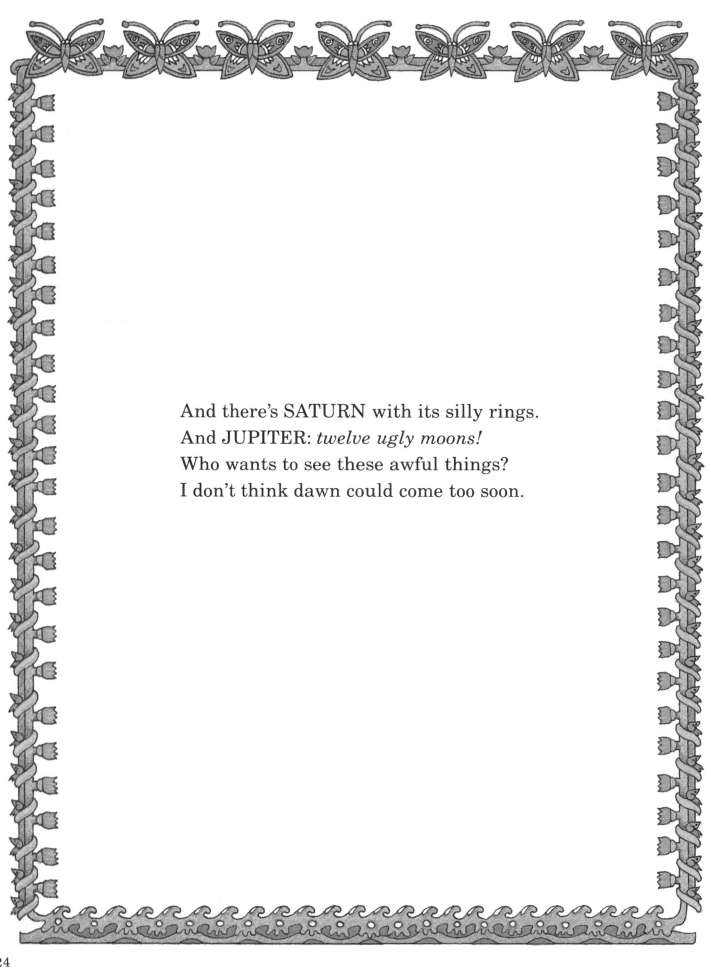

And there's SATURN with its silly rings.
And JUPITER: *twelve ugly moons!*
Who wants to see these awful things?
I don't think dawn could come too soon.

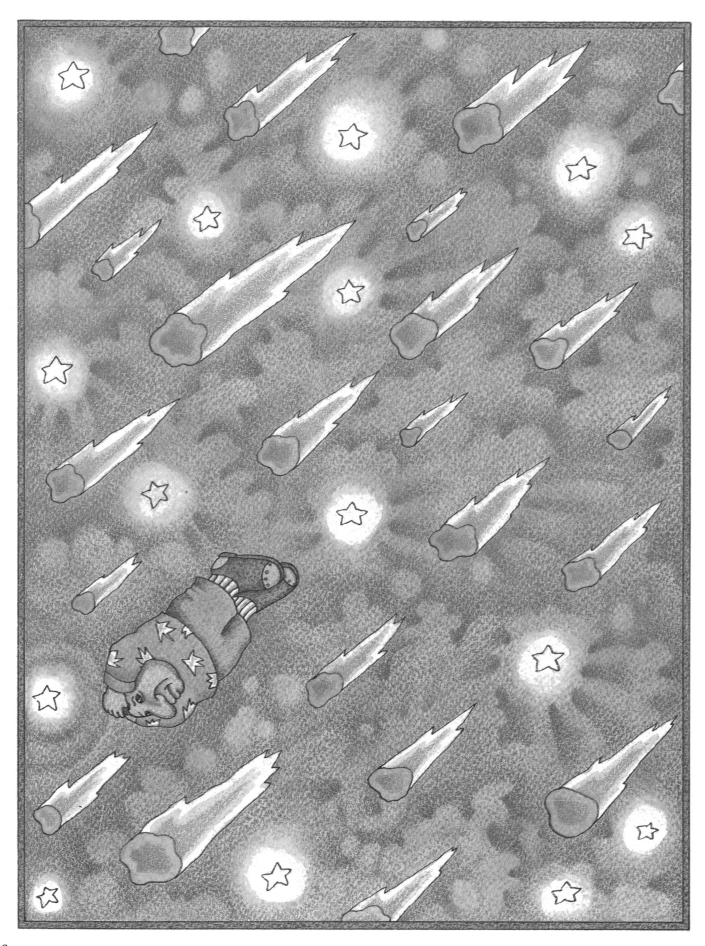

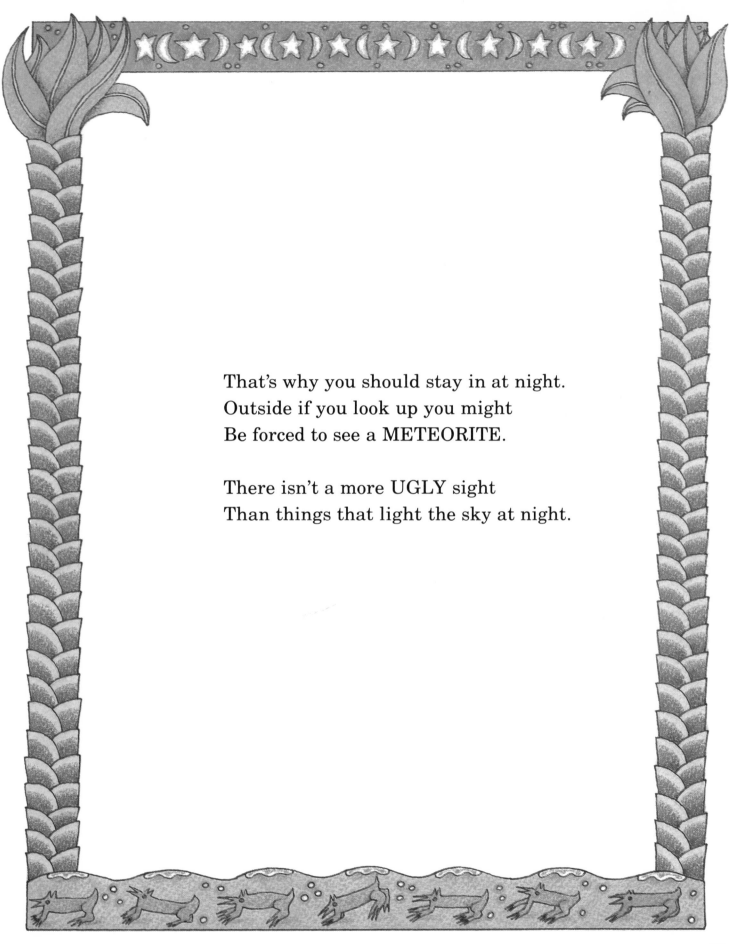

That's why you should stay in at night.
Outside if you look up you might
Be forced to see a METEORITE.

There isn't a more UGLY sight
Than things that light the sky at night.

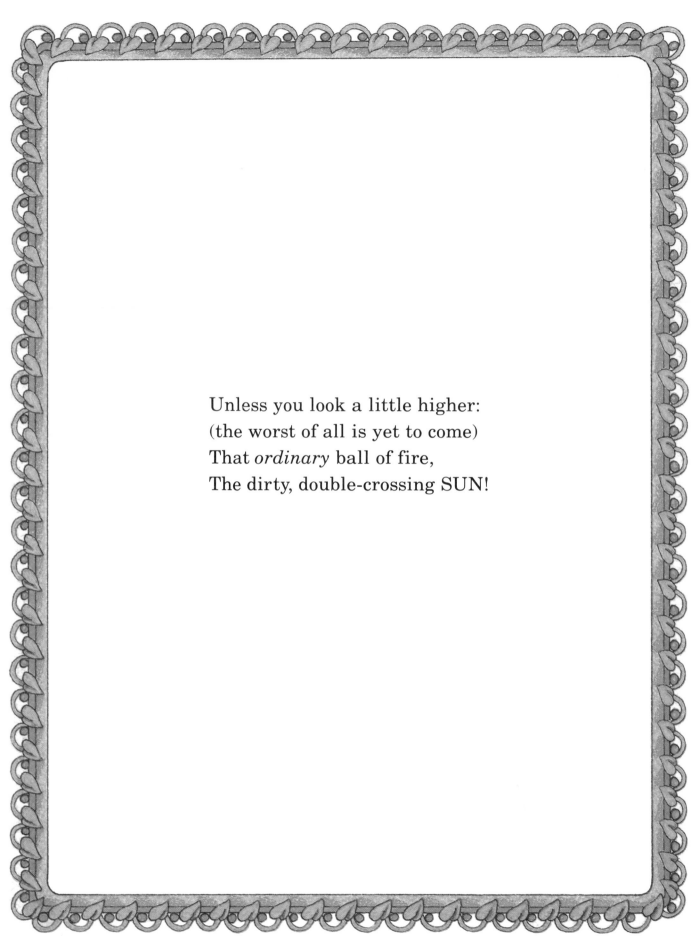

Unless you look a little higher:
(the worst of all is yet to come)
That *ordinary* ball of fire,
The dirty, double-crossing SUN!

At dawn he always wakes you up
When you'd much rather sleep instead.
But then at night he lets you down,
And off you go straight back to bed.

In winter he's not hot enough.
In summertime he burns your nose
And makes you wear a bathing suit.
Put mothballs in your winter clothes.

Of course, he's nothing you can *see*.
The SUN is much too bright himself.
He uses all his energy
To let us see everything else!

So you don't need an UGLY BOOK.
All you have to do is *look!*